To Mrs. Hart's Behavior Unit,
and to all the children who need a little extra guidance.

www.mascotbooks.com

The Supplies of Room Nine Learn to Shine

For more information, please contact:
Mascot Books
620 Herndon Parkway #320
Herndon, VA 20170
info@mascotbooks.com

Library of Congress Control Number: 2017915434

CPSIA Code: PRT0218A
ISBN-13:978-1-68401-476-7

Printed in the United States

The Supplies of Room Nine Learn to Shine

by Jessie Lewis

illustrated by Nidhom

The morning bell rings in room nine,
And all the school supplies are excited to play!
They've been waiting for this all summer long,
Sitting nice and still all night and day!

It's a day they wouldn't miss!
Time at last for all kinds
    of fun.
There were crafts,
    games, and love from
    their friends.
Here they all come with
    a skip and a run!

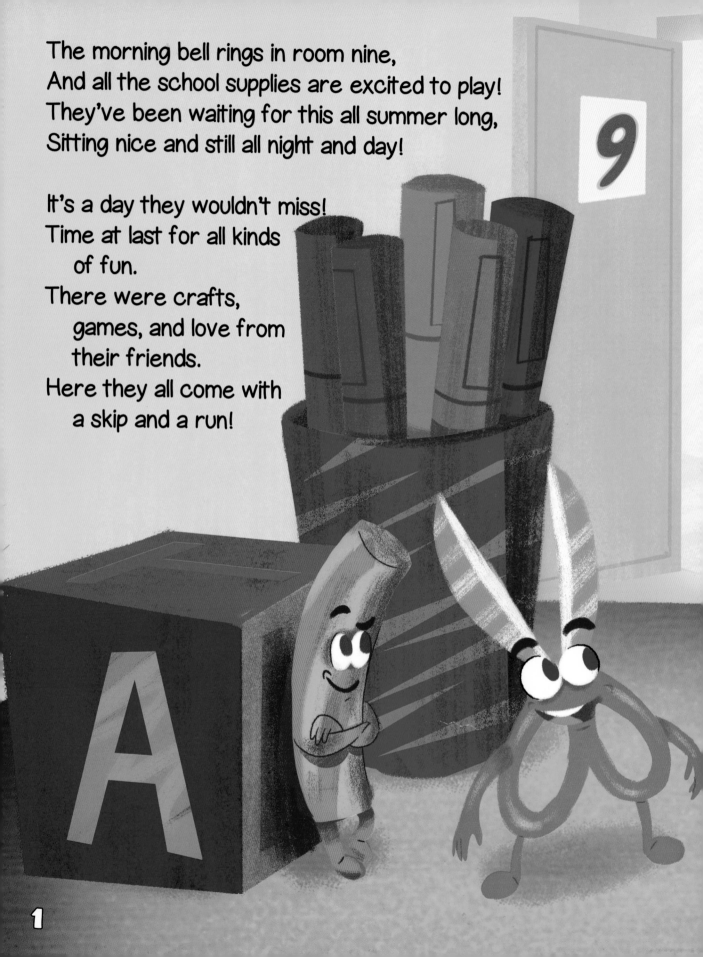

2

One boy grabbed little Rosie Crayon,
And started coloring a picture bold and grand.
Rosie Crayon's pink color cried out with joy!
Another girl snatched five crayons in one tiny hand!

All the markers waved goodbye as they were carried off.
Soon their bright colors would scribble the children's names.

Time passed quickly as they all played,
Enjoying their art, crafts, and games.

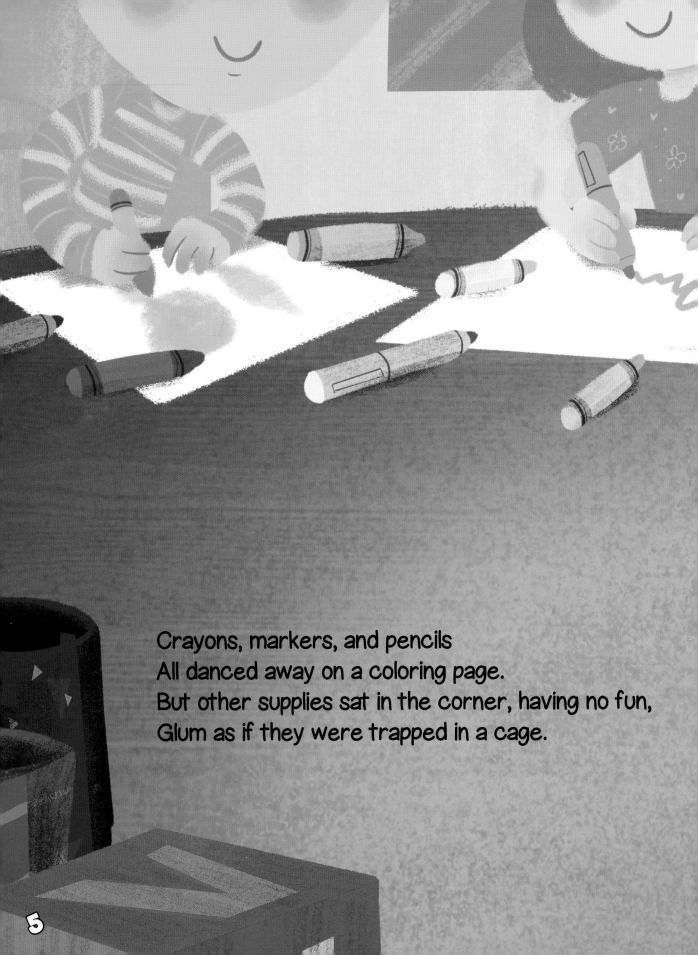

Crayons, markers, and pencils
All danced away on a coloring page.
But other supplies sat in the corner, having no fun,
Glum as if they were trapped in a cage.

No one wanted to play with Red Hot Scissors.
"He's sharp and dangerous!" everyone said.
"He is pointy and easily angered,
And will tear the work to shreds!"

No one wanted to play with Gilly Glue,
For she was super sticky as could be.
She would destroy all the art, they thought.
One touch from her, and they'd never be free.

Red Hot Scissors fumed with anger,
"It's not fair! I want to create like the crayons!"
Gilly Glue whined, "I just want to have fun."
Tears came to her eyes as she looked on.

Twisty Eraser Top saw them moping
And mocked their sad faces.
"All you do is destroy things!
You belong back in your cases!"

Fumes of anger spewed out of Red's handles,
And suddenly everyone was in danger.
He was destroying everything he saw,
As he violently released his anger.

Gilly Glue wailed in the corner out of fear and sadness,
"This won't make the kids want to play!"
But Red Hot Scissors refused to listen.
His anger continued, while all the crayons backed away.

No one knew what to do
Until Rosie Crayon had a thought.
She slid a piece of paper across the table,
And the other crayons held it in the right spot.

Red Hot Scissors wove in and out of the colored sheets
As stars and triangles floated to the ground.
Gilly Glue shrieked with fear,
"He's destroying the paper! He needs to calm down!"

"Be patient, Gilly," Rosie said,
"You'll see in just a bit."
Cutting the paper soothed Red Hot Scissors
And his frantic motions began to quit.

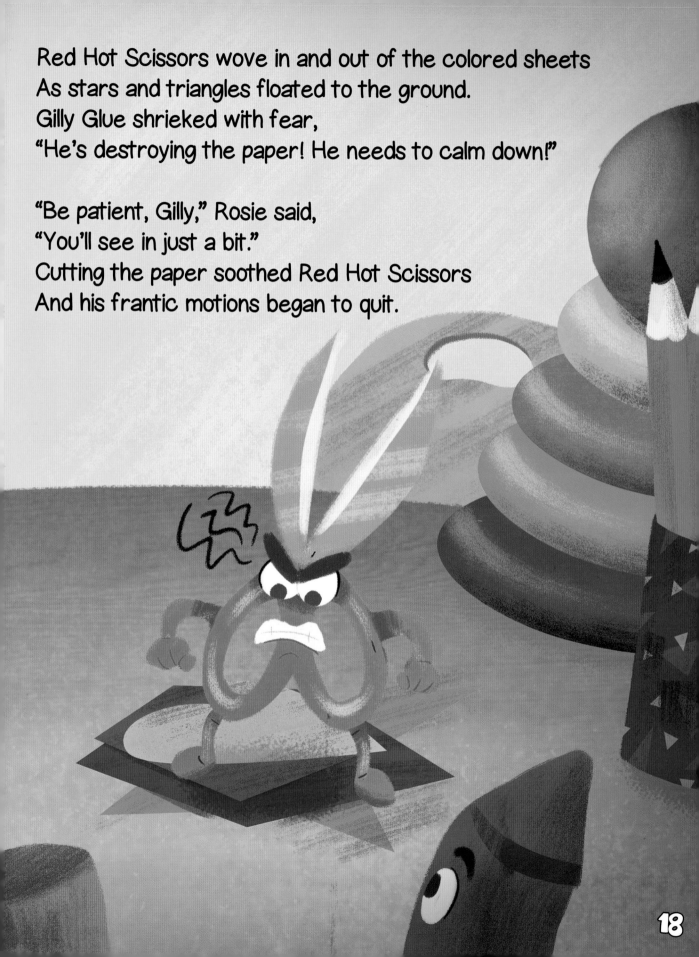

18

The paper sat in pieces on the table,
But then Rosie lifted up what he'd made.
The paper had turned into a beautiful masterpiece,
With elegant paper figures in a parade.

Red Hot Scissors was struck with tears,
For he had thought no child would ever want to play with him.
But when he saw what he had made,
Happiness filled him to the brim.

20

Red Hot Scissors became an artist,
And all the other supplies were tickled with delight.
Gilly Glue collected the scraps of paper,
And glued them together to help make a stunning sight.

When the children arrived the next morning,
They were surprised to find a colorfully crafted room nine.

Red Hot Scissors and Gilly Glue were no longer in the corner.
They were art supplies that had learned to shine!

About the Author

Jessie is studying Early Childhood and Special Education at Mercer University, where she is a member of the Service Scholars program, Mercer Educators in Action, and volunteers with the Boys and Girls Club of Central Georgia. She discovered her passion for working with children with special needs after volunteering in a Behavior Unit at Britton Elementary School in Hilliard, Ohio. Through this experience, she noticed the numerous challenges students with special needs face and wrote this book to help those students conquer those challenges and recognize their spectacular and unique qualities. It aligns with the "zones of regulation" that are often used in Behavior Classes. For every copy sold, Jessie will donate a copy to schools and organizations that help children in need.

To learn more about Jessie and *The Supplies of Room Nine Learn to Shine*, check out her website at:
jessicalewis83.wixsite.com/learningexpress